The Hill Street Five

Written by Jillian Powell

Illustrated by John Lund

Collins

Who's in this story?

Listen and say

Download the audio at www.collins.co.uk/839794

Dan

Matt

Bill

May

Lily

This is our street. It is on a hill.
I live here. My name is Bill.
There is a big sports centre at the top.
There are lots of houses and a nice sweet shop.

This is my house. It's number three.

In the garden, there's an old apple tree.

This is my favourite blue football.

Sometimes I kick it at this wall.

My friend Dan lives at number four.
His house has got a big green door.

This is Dan's football shirt.

Our friend May lives at number five.
There is a black car on the drive.

These are May's football boots.

May's best friend Lily lives at number eight.

Her house has got a blue garden gate.

Our friend Matt's house is sixteen, near the top.

He lives next to our favourite sweet shop.

We know many people on the hill.

At number thirteen is Mark, at fifteen is Jill.

We know Jill's father from the sweet shop.

We know the Smith family at fourteen, near the top.

On Wednesdays, we meet after three.
Dan, Matt and Lily, May and me.

At the sports centre we play a
football game.
The Hill Street Five is our name.

We dream of football night and day.
All we want to do is play.
But today the game was not a lot of fun.
They scored six goals. We scored none!

Then we walk home and Matt asks Lily,
"Who lives there?" She says, "Don't
be silly.
No people live next door to May.
Read the sign! They put it there today."

Number seven looks sad and sorry.

Then one day we see a lorry.

"They are stopping at number seven," says May.

"Let's see what's on the lorry,' I say.

Four men are working in two pairs.
They carry boxes up the stairs.

We see two chairs, a table and a bed.
"Look!" says Lily. "Everything is red!"

Next comes a piano, then two bikes.
We know the colour that he likes!
Who is moving next to May?
"Let's ask them who it is," I say.

The men are stopping for some tea,
"*He's* moving here," one man says to me.
The man points to a fast red car.
"That's his! He was a football star."

The man gets out and waves to us.

We know him. He is famous!

He played football for the Reds as number eleven.

Now he lives at house number seven!

He sees our ball and comes to say,
"Can I play football with you one day?"
"Wow!" says Lily. "Wow!" says Dan.
I say loudly, "Yes, you can!"

He shows us how to kick the ball.
We throw. We score. We learn it all.
We want to be the best we can,
Matt, May and Lily, me and Dan.

On Wednesday night, he watches us play.
He says, "We can win the cup one day!"

Now we are winning every game.
The Little Reds is our new name!

Picture dictionary

Listen and repeat

football boots   football shirt   football shorts

football socks   kick   score a goal

sports centre   throw   win a cup

1 Look and order the story

2 Listen and say

Collins

Published by Collins
An imprint of HarperCollins*Publishers*
Westerhill Road
Bishopbriggs
Glasgow
G64 2QT

HarperCollins*Publishers*
1st Floor, Watermarque Building
Ringsend Road
Dublin 4
Ireland

William Collins' dream of knowledge for all began with the publication of his first book in 1819.

A self-educated mill worker, he not only enriched millions of lives, but also founded a flourishing publishing house. Today, staying true to this spirit, Collins books are packed with inspiration, innovation and practical expertise. They place you at the centre of a world of possibility and give you exactly what you need to explore it.

10 9 8 7 6 5 4 3 2

ISBN 978-0-00-839794-4

Collins® and COBUILD® are registered trademarks of HarperCollins*Publishers* Limited

www.collins.co.uk/elt

Author: Jillian Powell
Illustrator: John Lund (Beehive)
Series editor: Rebecca Adlard
Publishing manager: Lisa Todd
Product managers: Jennifer Hall and Caroline Green
In-house editor: Alma Puts Keren
Project manager: Emily Hooton
Editor: Matthew Hancock
Proofreaders: Natalie Murray and Michael Lamb
Cover designer: Kevin Robbins
Typesetter: 2Hoots Publishing Services Ltd
Audio produced by id audio, London
Reading guide author: Emma Wilkinson
Production controller: Rachel Weaver
Printed and bound by: GPS Group, Slovenia

MIX
Paper from
responsible sources

FSC
www.fsc.org
FSC™ C007454

Download the audio for this book and a reading guide for parents and teachers at www.collins.co.uk/839794